The Red Jacket Mix-Up

By ARI HILL
Illustrated by BRUCE LEMERISE

For Mary V. Miller

A GOLDEN BOOK • NEW YORK
Western Publishing Company, Inc., Racine, Wisconsin 53404

"Bobby," said Mrs. Fizz to her grandson, "this is our
lucky day. The Big Store is having a sale, and you need
a new spring jacket."

The snow was still on the ground, so Mrs. Fizz and Bobby bundled up in their warm winter clothes. They took the bus downtown to the Big Store.

At the store, everything seemed to be on sale. And everyone in town seemed to be there.

"Bobby," said Mrs. Fizz, "why don't you take off your jacket? It will be easier to try things on."

So Bobby took off his red down jacket and put it on top of a rack.

BOYS' SHOP

Bobby tried on a green jacket, a blue jacket, and finally a tan jacket.

"That's it," said Mrs. Fizz.

"I like it, too," said Bobby.

While the clerk wrapped up his new jacket, Bobby took his red one off the rack and put it on again.

Bobby and Mrs. Fizz went over to the toy department. They watched some robots that changed into cars race along a track.

Suddenly, Bobby felt his jacket move. "It must be my imagination," he thought.

But then it happened again. And whatever was moving was in his pocket!

Then Bobby noticed something strange—his pocket was partway open. He always kept it zipped up tight so his lucky elephant coin wouldn't fall out.

Bobby unzipped the pocket and tried to peek inside. Out jumped a large green frog. Bobby and Mrs. Fizz stood open-mouthed as the frog jumped from table to table and landed on the railing of the DOWN escalator.

"Let's go get him!" shouted Bobby.

As they rode down after the frog, Mrs. Fizz said,
"Why did you bring that frog to this crowded store?"
"I didn't," said Bobby. "The only thing I had in my
pocket this morning was my elephant coin. I must have
somebody else's jacket. We'd better find that frog!"

When they reached the floor below, Bobby hurried
off to see if the frog had gone down the next escalator.
But Mrs. Fizz said, "I doubt that the frog cares much
for escalators. Let's look around here."

They walked into the bath department. There was a
large bathtub surrounded by soap dishes, cups, and
stacks of towels and washcloths—all with frog designs.

Bobby and Mrs. Fizz searched carefully, even among
the shower curtains, but they didn't find a single live frog.

They headed into the fancy food department. A sign said SPECIAL—LOUISIANA FROGS' LEGS.

"Uh-oh," said Bobby.

He and his grandma took a quick look around. Luckily, the frog wasn't there.

DUCK
EGGS

Next door, in kitchenware, a man in a chef's hat was giving a cooking lesson.

Suddenly a little girl shrieked, "Look! A frog!"

Sure enough, the frog was leaping across the counter.

Bobby and Mrs. Fizz followed the frog past displays of dishes, vases, and giftware. Then they lost him—right in front of a table of frog candlesticks.

Then Bobby saw one of the candlesticks move. He grabbed it.

"Now I've got you!" he said, picking up the frog and plopping it into his pocket.

"Goodness!" was all Mrs. Fizz could say.

But Bobby said, "Great, now we have the frog back.
Only it's some other kid's frog—and his jacket, too.
Where are my lucky coin and my jacket? What will we do?"

"Come on back to the jacket department," said Mrs.
Fizz. "We'll have another look around." So off they went.

They looked and looked but couldn't find Bobby's jacket anywhere.

"Let's talk to that sales clerk," said Bobby. "Maybe he can help us."

"Why, yes," said the clerk. "I remember another boy with a jacket just like yours. He was here with his mother. She had short, dark hair."

"Do you know which way they went?" asked Bobby.

"Let me see," said the clerk. "I think the boy said he was hungry."

"Maybe they went down to the restaurant," said Bobby.

So Bobby and Mrs. Fizz hurried downstairs to the restaurant. There were lots of kids with red down jackets, and lots of mothers with short, dark hair.

Mrs. Fizz took a deep breath. She walked into the center of the room and banged a glass with a spoon until everyone was looking at her. Bobby's face turned as red as his jacket.

Then Mrs. Fizz said loudly, "Bobby has a red down jacket and a frog that don't belong to him. Someone has Bobby's jacket. Is it anyone here?"

Everyone looked, but no one had Bobby's jacket.

"There's only one thing left to do," Mrs. Fizz said to Bobby. She steered him to the Lost and Found office As they entered, they heard a boy's shaky voice saying, "Th-the frog's name is Fred...."

"Is this Fred?" asked Bobby, holding up the frog and grinning.

"Fred!" the boy said happily. He looked at Bobby. "This must be your elephant coin."

"My coin!" said Bobby. "I always knew it would bring me luck."

After lunch, Mrs. Fizz asked Bobby, "Are you ready to do some more shopping now?"

"Sure," Bobby answered. "What do you have to buy?"

"I could use a new spring jacket, too," his grandma said.

"Okay," said Bobby. "Just one thing, though—let me hold your winter coat when you try things on!"